KU-376-457

Jane Gardam

KIT

Illustrated by William Geldart

Julia MacRae Books

A division of Franklin Watts

For Felicity

First published in Great Britain 1983 by
Julia MacRae Books
A division of Franklin Watts
12a Golden Square, London, W1R 4BA
and Franklin Watts Inc.
387 Park Avenue South, New York 10016

British Library Cataloguing in Publication Data
Gardam, Jane
Kit
I. Title
823'.914 [J] PZ7
ISBN 0–86203–132–X UK edition
ISBN 0–531–03763–0 US edition
Library of Congress Catalog Card No. 83–61538

Printed in Great Britain by
Robert Hartnoll, Bodmin

Contents

Also in the Redwing Series

YOUR GUESS IS AS GOOD AS MINE Bernard Ashley
TIGERS FOREVER Ruskin Bond

1

The Kit was not a kitten. She was a girl. She was seven and she was called The Kit because she was a baby. If you are a baby when you are seven – that is to say, if you are still crying over just this and that (such as juicy black beetles walking out from under the sink, or getting your new shoe in a clart) then you are a Kit.

Not if you cry over big things. Not if you cry over lambs going to market or the pig-killer coming. Farming fathers and mothers often mind about these things themselves even though they put on strong faces. Farming mothers often take their children down to the beck to wobble on stones and splash and put hands under ice-cold waterfalls or twizzle about in a rubber dinghy under low branches along the bank, when the pig-killer comes.

The Kit's mother did anyway.

But what mothers and fathers say round about The Kit's farm when a child cries for nothing is, "So this is The Kit is it?" They say it in voices that mean they don't think much of Kits.

When you are brave, however, and stop crying, and wipe your face up and give a stamp at the black beetles or sensibly take off your shoe and clean the clart away (a clart by the way is a cow-pat), then they say, "*That's* a good girl," and they half sing,

"Is this the *Cat*
That was the *Kit*
Before she went to *London*?"

The Kit, whose real name was Catherine, and Kitty for short, hardly ever got this said to her: for she really was a bit of a misery.

"I don't know why she's such a moaning minnie," her father used to say. "She's the dead opposite of our Lisa."

"Isn't she?" he used to add, tickling baby

Lisa under the chin; and baby Lisa would wave her spoon and scatter mush about the carpet, and thunder her heels against the foot-rest on her baby chair, and grin like a monkey, and smear food on her scarlet cheeks, and laugh until her blue eyes nearly disappeared, and very messy The Kit thought she was.

Nothing seemed to upset Lisa. Once she even fell out of her chair on to her head and when they picked her up she was still laughing.

"There's my little cat," their mother had said, hugging her. "My little cat's got to London already."

"Who wants to go to London?" said The Kit. She didn't know what London was but she knew that she didn't want to go to it.

She didn't want to go anywhere. She wanted to sit in the hay and eat apples, or make a cave in the bracken above the farm, and plant peas and carrots even if the sheep came and ate

them. She wanted to balance about on the stone walls and pounce down and watch the lambs leap in the air like electric shocks; or creep up near the cows and hear the huge tearing sounds they made with their tongues, tugging out the grass. She liked cows and they did not frighten her. She even liked the bull rather, and used to lean over the gate at him and stroke his huge knobbly forehead, and he would blow loud noises at her and swing his head about. Her

father would shout, "That'll *do* now," and come running, seeing her nearly toppling over the field gate. He would whisk The Kit up in his arms and roar at the bull who would roar back at him.

"I don't know," said The Kit's father, "I've known some daft youths, but never like this Kit. Cry, cry over midges and then goes stroking a demon like that Geoffrey!"

Geoffrey was the bull's name. He had bright, angry eyes all his waking hours, which seemed to be always. Even at night you could hear him thumping about in the dreadful, dark hull (a hull is a stone shed), which was supposed to be his bedroom but where he often spent his days too, and if The Kit crept up to peep through the hole in his door-sneck (a sneck is a latch), there was his slimy, rattly nose-ring and his pink, wet nostril half an inch from her eye. The Kit hated the bull's hull, and the bull's slimy nose-ring and the bull's pink, wet nostril, but she loved the woolly part of his nose and his forehead and tickled it through the sneck-hole very happily; and Geoffrey used to fling away and snuffle and shout like the baby did when their father tickled her chin.

"Leave over tormenting that bull," her mother would shout. "Come and help me jam these plums."

But The Kit hated jamming plums. They made her hands sticky and got everywhere, even on the soles of her shoes and then the shoes made crackling noises and left plummy tracks all over the kitchen floor, and her mother said, "Oh, give *over* then Kitty. Lisa could do better."

"She's got no sort of *gumption*," her mother used to say at school to Miss Bell, but Miss Bell would say, "Nonsense Margaret." (Miss Bell had taught The Kit's mother too, long ago.) "I think that Catherine will give us all a surprise one of these days." And she let The Kit sit at the back of the class and do Drawing in Reading – because The Kit could read like anything, anyway. The Kit would draw Geoffrey thumping about in a dark and dreadful cave, trying to get at the carrots and peas which the smug sheep were eating, his eyes giving off space rockets of despair.

2

After a late, cold lambing, hay-time came early that year. Something magic happened to the weather and as early as March it grew hot as summer holidays – and hotter. The grass grew up bright and green. It blew in the warm wind, and turned golden and dry and not even too full of flowers for good hay. All kinds of jobs got left that were usually done in the pause after the lambs had come – like the straightening of the stone roof-slates which had slipped sideways in the wind; the building up of field walls knocked over by snow; and the small repairs to the farm buildings, like the door-sneck inside the bull's hull which had come to the end of its life, after being eaten by frost.

"Are you going to mend that *sneck*?" The Kit's mother asked The Kit's father again and again. "It's a disgrace."

"It's no disgrace," said he. "It's lasted these hundred years. None of us is going to be as useful by that age."

"Well, it's no use at all now," said The Kit's mother. "It's sunk down in the muck of the hull – and that's another disgrace. It's three foot deep in muck, that hull, but it'd not take half a day to clear it."

"There's no half days to spare," said The Kit's father, sniffing the sky. They were all standing in the first big hay-field. The Kit was holding her mother's hand. The baby on her father's arm was bouncing and singing and conducting an orchestra. "I've the feel we could start hay any time. Even tomorrow."

"Well, that hull door isn't safe. It's going to give trouble."

"Never it will. It's only from inside you can't get out. There's no trouble from outside getting in. You can still shut the bull up safe, which is all that matters. It's no loss that he can't lift the latch on the inside himself, and get out."

"No – but someone else might want to lift the latch from inside and get out. Someone could get shut inside with him. Someone taking in his feed."

"Lunatics maybe."

"No. Not lunatics. Me. If you were away off somewhere and Kitty at school, I could be trapped in there, no one to hear me shout but the baby. There's often no one up here all day except the postman, and he doesn't come every day. I'd be trapped if that door swung to when I was feeding up. Or Kitty could be trapped if she was round there calling."

"She'd never go in, would you Kit? Not in that slathery muck of a hull."

"No," said The Kit, shivering, "I wouldn't. I hate the bull's hull. I just talk to him through the sneck-hole."

"There'll be no talking to anyone tomorrow, through sneck-holes or what-all," said her father. "It'll be all hands to hay-time."

And it was. For six days The Kit's parents and The Kit worked and worked. The Kit minded Lisa and ran back and forth to the field with sandwiches. She got Lisa in and out of her chair, and in and out of her play-pen, spooned her dinner in to her mouth, and washed her face afterwards. She made tea, put it in a can, ran to the field again with it, kept the stove going for hot water for baths, answered the telephone, fed the chickens and the pigs and the

sheep-dogs and watched her parents after they had fed the calves and the bull (which was grown-up work) falling asleep as they ate their own supper at night.

She didn't go to school. There was no question of that. All down the Dale other, richer farmers were working, too, some of them with expensive machines in the fields and five and six helpers, but even in these fields there were quite big children missing school and working at the hay.

"Miss Bell'll be furious," said The Kit.

"She always was," said her mother. "Hay-time."

"She says it's slave labour," said The Kit.

"She always did," said her mother.

3

The weather was so wonderful that after six days of cutting and baling the hay, it was dry and sweet as lavender bags and The Kit's father said, "There's miracles about. I've never known a year like it. We can elevate tomorrow."

Elevating is lifting the hay blocks up into the stone barns for winter. Rich farmers – most farmers – have electric, caterpillarish machines for this and it is easy; but poor farmers have to toss the blocks up with a fork from a pick-up below. It is very hard work and gets harder as you get nearer the end, because the smaller the pile gets in the farm-yard, the higher you have to toss it up. The Kit's father took over the hardest work right up to the finish, but, when it was nearly all done, The Kit and her mother who had been catching and stacking, which is very hard, too, looked out of the high barn door above his head with sore eyes and sneezing noses and aching arms and pitiable faces.

"What's this then?" said he.

"We're done. We can't finish. We've got to stop stacking," said The Kit's mother.

"Stand aside then," he said, and he tossed up the last bales. "Come on. Down the ladder and I'll up and finish them."

They came down the ladder and up went he, and in the dark of the barn he heaved and jig-sawed the last big, heavy bales of hay into place until all was tidy and safe, and the barn was full.

Then he took a step back to look at how beautiful it all was and fell out of the high barn door in to the farm-yard far below and broke his leg!

You never heard such a noise except perhaps from Geoffrey the bull when he'd been shut up

in the hull too long in fine weather. The Kit's father was a big strong man and when he fell on anything it was usually the thing he fell on that broke, not he. But farm-yards don't break, and if this one had not still had a good layer of hay on it more of The Kit's father than just his leg would have broken, and he wouldn't have been able to roar at all.

The Kit's mother rushed to the telephone while The Kit hugged Lisa tight, and chickens, sheep-dogs, calves and Geoffrey clamoured for their supper in vain.

Soon from far away, The Kit could see the ambulance coming and then ambulance men walked firmly across the yard with a stretcher.

"Take away that stretcher," roared The Kit's father, "I'm not leaving this farm."

"You can't stay lying there in the hay," said the ambulance men. "You'll have broken something. You'll have to be x-rayed."

"X-ray me here," commanded The Kit's father with rolling, Geoffrey-like eyes, his beard twitching with rage and pain. The ambulance men talked together and went away, and soon another van was to be seen winding its way up the dale, with the Doctor's car ahead of it.

The Doctor took no notice at all of The Kit's father's roars – simply directed the x-ray men to help him into the house with him. Then, after the x-ray men had taken the photographs to the van to develop, and a lot of telephoning had gone on, and The Kit's father had said about a hundred times that he would not leave the farm, the Doctor said, "Very well – but if you stay here you'll not be able to move. Maybe not for six weeks. You'll have to be put in *traction.*"

"Tied in my bed?"

"Yes."

"But where I can keep an eye on things?"

"We can really manage on our own –" said The Kit's mother.

"WHERE I CAN KEEP AN EYE ON THINGS?" roared The Kit's father.

"If you must," said the Doctor, "though I'm glad the telephone is halfway up the stairs, where you won't be able to get at it."

"Put me in traction then," he said, shutting his eyes and pointing his beard at the ceiling.

Then The Kit and Lisa and their mother went for a walk by the beck, far out of the way, and Lisa laughed the whole time and their mother cried and The Kit thought that this was being a very long day.

4

"Six weeks," said the Doctor, when they got back. "It will be six weeks at the very least. More like eight."

"Margaret, have you fed that *bull*?" rang out from the big kitchen. They had put The Kit's father in the kitchen on a bed, to be near the centre of things and to save getting him up the stairs.

"No. Not yet. I –"

"He's not to move," said the Doctor. "But you needn't worry. He's tied by the leg so he can't stir. You can see. There's a big weight attached to him. You'll have no trouble. I've given him something to calm him down."

"HAVE YOU FED THEM ANIMALS?"

bellowed The Kit's father.

"Not yet, for goodness sake!" wept her mother.

"I'll be round tomorrow. And every day," said the Doctor, "and bear up."

"Oh yes," he added by his car, pointing at The Kit, "this one's for school tomorrow. She needs a bit of peace."

"She's needed here," roared her father.

"She is *not*," said the Doctor.

"I can't manage without her. Not with the baby," said her mother. "Up here it's not like in a village. There's no neighbours."
"Oh, I'll stay," said The Kit, "I don't care."
"Well, I do," said the Doctor, "I say school."

And the next day she did go to school and Miss Bell was very glad to see her, but the day after that her desk was empty again.
For the magic weather had gone.
It was as if, when the Kit's father had fallen out of the hay barn, the sun had fallen out of the sky.
First of all a wind began to blow. Then great clouds came sweeping in from the head of the Dale and swirled all over it. Then the whole sky darkened and the real rain began – great swinging curtains of it that turned the little roads into young rivers, the becks into brown torrents and the river down the Dale bottom into flood-waters which spread over the fields like pale, frothy lakes. At the end of the road, down from the farm, a rushing stream appeared in less than an hour, so deep that it

covered the flimsy wooden foot-bridge that two days ago had been as dry as matches. "The bridge is covered," said The Kit, coming back from trying to go to school, "so I couldn't get."

"Oh dear," said her mother, very pleased. "Here then. Just get your father's breakfast while I get on with my washing. Though where to hang it out – round his bed in the kitchen, likely. If ever the Doctor gets here we'll get him to carry the television in here. It'll make evenings easier at least."

"I can't watch with *Father*," said The Kit.

"You'll have to or I'll run mad," said her mother. "Oh and when you've got his breakfast, set Lisa on her pot."

"*Must* I?"

"Yes, and why not Madam?"

"I hate it. I hate everything." She began to cry.

"Oh, heaven help us," wept her mother back.

"Bah, bah, bah, *hoop*-la," sang the baby.

"Where's my *breakfast*?" roared their father. "Have you seen to the calves? Will someone come here and scratch my foot – I've an itch to it."

"I won't, I won't," cried The Kit.

The kitchen steamed with wet washing, the rain bucketed down outside and neglected Geoffrey, in the bull's hull, swung his head and thought of murder.

5

But it was over a fortnight later that the most fearful thing happened, just when you would have thought that everyone would have been settling down. The rain had turned to no more than a cold, fine mizzle, the Doctor was still coming once a week up the hill, though it had to be on foot, and, though no visitors had yet ventured up to the farm, the foot-bridge was quite possible in wellingtons. The Kit's father was not in so much pain and had begun to watch Breakfast Television, which he thought was marvellous, and the baby was as good as ever. Nicest of all, the people who telephoned from round about were full of praise for the whole family for being so clever as to get their hay safe in before the storm – "Grand young farmers," they said. "And even the little lass is helping."

The trouble came on a Tuesday morning when The Kit and her mother suddenly got furious with one another.

Neither of them knew how it started. Nor did The Kit's father, who for once was dumbfounded for nearly half a minute. Nor did the baby, who fell silent in the middle of a coo.

The truth was that The Kit and her mother had been crammed in too close to each other for too long and had grown a bit peculiar – rather like when you look at yourself in a mirror for a long time. They were both tired of the inside of the house and they both knew that The Kit ought to be back at school.

This drowning wet morning, with a bad-tempered wind blowing, The Kit had been told to go and get the pig bucket and take it to the pig, and she came running in to say that she had seen a shabby, wet rat eating out of it and she began to scream and cry.

"Rat!" roared her father, and her mother

joined in, "Really Kitty – afraid of a rat! And you living on a farm. What if it was Africa with lions and tigers?"

"I *love* lions and tigers." The Kit stopped wailing to say, "I hate mucky, foul, filthy rats."

"That's enough, you're frightening Lisa."

"And messy, clever-*cats*." And she kicked

the baby's bouncing-chair.

"That'll do!"

"And mucky, foul, filthy old *dumps*."

"Kitty!"

"Like this one. This farm. All mucky. And wet. Like the bull's hull. Like *you*."

And before anything could be done or said she was gone from the house, down the yard, through the trees and out of sight.

Silence fell in the kitchen.

After a moment or so her mother went to the window and then to the door and looked through the cold rain that blew in at her. "She'll be back," she said.

"Aye, she'll be back," said her father. "Daft young 'ape-orth."

The Kit's mother shut the door and dried her face and hair on a tea-towel, "Them rats," she said.

"There's rats everywhere," said The Kit's father. "Plenty in towns. London's full of them it's said. Only difference is you don't see them in London. They slink about secret.

Underground.''

''Well, that might be better.''

''I'd sooner have things out in the open.''

''*I* never liked rats,'' said The Kit's mother. ''Nor yet dirt. Rats mean dirt.''

''Never. There'll be rats in Buckingham Palace.''

''That I'd doubt. Rats brought The Great Plague. D'you remember drawing it for Miss Bell?''

''Aye. But rats is natural beings. Live and let live. That Kitty's soft. She can't think.''

''She's young yet for thinking,'' said her mother. ''Mind that bull's hull *is* a sight. There's no way but I'll have to get on with cleaning it out myself I suppose.''

''That you'll not. That I forbid,'' and The Kit's father began to thump the bed and thunder at his strung-up leg.

''Well, I'll have to feed and water the bull anyway,'' she said, ''and the rest of them.'' She finished the washing-up and put on a scarf, a macintosh and a sacking apron over the macintosh. ''I'll do the pig and calves and

Geoffrey and then I'll away up to the gimmers.'' Gimmers are last year's lambs, teen-agers, and often take quite a bit of seeing to, like teen-aged people. These gimmers were on a high bit of fell over a mile away.

''I'll be a while,'' she said. ''Are you all right? Kitty'll be back in a minute.''

''Aye, as right as I'll be till I get these strings off.'' He lay back and closed his eyes. Lisa strapped in her chair had done the same and The Kit's mother riddled the stove, put on her wellingtons and went out.

She took the rat-eaten pig bucket and fed the pig. Then she made up the milk buckets and fed the calves.

She fed the chickens.

She went to the barn for the bull's fodder and the bucket of water to put in his trough. Both arms full, she went to the hull. She had to kick the door open behind her to get in, and leave it standing wide, but she knew that the bull would make no move to get out with his dinner coming. "Hello Geoffrey," she said.

Geoffrey was standing quietly, up above his ankles in his treacly black carpet. He had a puzzled, thoughtful look, not unfriendly. He has his kindly side, she thought, he makes a lot of noise but he's a pleasant enough young bull. She tossed hay up into the manger and Geoffrey came squidging across. He leaned against her for a moment and sighed and then began to eat the hay. "Poor lad," she said and scratched his iron forehead. "What a life. Shut up in here in the dark. Not even knowing it's not for ever. You don't even know if you'll ever get out in the fields again, do you young Geoffrey? Don't even know that things change and the sun comes out? And not a soul to talk to. No wonder bulls go mad." She scratched his thick, red, woolly neck as he stretched it up to the hay. "They say you can never trust a bull," she said, "not even one you've reared. But you're a grand lad, Geoffrey. You're right soft really." She stepped back, slipped in the deep mire, caught her wellington on the bucket, which clanged loudly as it fell against the water trough, and Geoffrey reared away from the manger in fright.

At the same moment the wind slammed shut the broken hull door.

6

"I'm leaving," The Kit said to the foot-bridge, sploshing over it in her bedroom slippers. "*They*'ll see. I'm leaving home. I hate them."

She sploshed on.

"I'm going," she told a big hay-lorry that came fizzing out of the dark rain along the main road, soaking her to the waistline.

"To London, since that's what they want," she informed the school gate, through which somehow or other she seemed to be walking.

"Oh good," said Miss Bell. "Dear me, Catherine, you're a bit wet. Let's take off those bedroom slippers. Did you not have a coat? Here dry yourself and take off that dress. We'll find an overall."

"I'm all right."

"Thank you."

"Thank you."

"You're very late. We're half way through Reading."

"Can I sit at the back?"

"No. Today you do what the others do."

She read, taking her turn round the class. She read very well, too, with lots of expression, though she felt cold and shuddery even in the dry overall. At Break she said, "Can I stay in?"

"No. The rain has stopped. You're all to go out. Today you do what the others do."

So she stood about the yard. When they said "Is your Dad's leg better?" she said, "He's all right." The sun came out and made the puddles flash in the yard.

It was over an hour later that her father in his kitchen bed woke up, tried to stretch, squawked, and saw the sun.

"No Kitty," he said.

The kitchen was flooded with light and all the drops along the gutter pipe outside the window were shining like wet glass beads. They kept scattering in the wind and new ones gathered up again. It'll be wild up on the fell with them gimmers, he thought next. Margaret's taking a time. They're *both* taking a time. Twisting his head to see the clock he found it was well after mid-day. By – they *are* taking a time. I must have been asleep near two hours. Lisa he saw was awake and watching him, and seeing him awake, began to biff her heels against her chair-rest and laugh. Then she began to biff them harder. Rather fiercely.

"Dare say you're getting hungry, young lass. I know I am."

Outside the wind blew. Otherwise all was very quiet, for the bull's hull was a long way from the house.

At twelve-thirty, dinner-time, The Kit did not tidy up her books. When all the other children went pushing and shouting out of the room she sat on at her desk.

Miss Bell said, "Catherine?"

The Kit sat on.

Miss Bell came and sat at the next desk, and

tears moved down The Kit's face.

"Is something wrong?"

"No."

"No thank you."

"No thank you."

"Then go to your dinner."

"I went for my mother."

"I see. Today?"

"Yes. And they went for *me*. Both of them."

"I see."

"Then I ran away."

"Oh. I see. Then we must ring her up at once. She'll be very worried. She has plenty to worry about already. She'll have been on to the police by now."

"*She* won't worry about me." More tears rolled.

"I tell you, Catherine, that she will. I know your mother. I've known her since she was seven like you, and she was as like you as a twin, except she was more of a scaredy-cat."

"My *mother*!"

"She was a proper scaredy-cat. Or Kit. She was the biggest Kit ever."

"My *mother*! She's strong and brave as lions."

"No she isn't. Now, Catherine, I've decided something. I'm not on dinner-duty and I'm free until afternoon school. I'll just have a word, and then we'll get in my car and we'll go up to the farm and we'll put things right."

"I'm never going back. Not to the farm. Never. I'm going to London."

"London'll keep," said Miss Bell. "Just at present you're going home."

7

They had to walk to the foot-bridge and Miss Bell, who was old, said that she had not walked this hill in years and hoped that she would never have to do so again.

"Though the trouble's worth it once you're up," she said, puffing and blowing as they came out on to the open pasture. Everything shone in the new sunlight and turned the bare hay-fields below to electric green and the heather common above to rich and furry purple. The sheep stood bright and white, and the deep, muddy ruts in the lane shone silver. "Oh you live in a lovely place, Catherine," said Miss Bell.

"But whatever is *that*!" she said, reaching

for The Kit's hand.

A mixture of roars, howls, bellows and screams was rising from the farm and grew louder and louder as they hurried nearer. The Kit, rushing ahead into the kitchen, saw her father's rolling eyes and his hands desperately trying to free his broken leg from the Doctor's knots. Arching her back in her chair, black in the face, arms and legs aspread, the baby was roaring at last.

But "Oh help!" said The Kit, for the really frightful noise was not coming from the house at all.

The Kit was gone.

"Jonathan," said Miss Bell sternly to The Kit's father, "What is this about?" But "Quick – Quick," he shouted at her. "Get to the bull's hull. Margaret's shut in there."

"No – no – get to the *yard*, woman," he roared as Miss Bell turned vaguely towards the wrong door, "*Run.*"

And Miss Bell ran, tottering a little on the flagstoned yard, slipping on the bumpy cobbles. For the first time in her life she felt watery and frail and old. And also for the first time in her life she felt that she didn't know quite what to do.

The awful noise had stopped. The only noise now was from inside – The Kit's father shouting and shouting, "I thought she was with the gimmers. She may have been an hour in there. Two hours. Why didn't she shout? It's only the bull you can hear. She'll be trampled! She's been trampled already! She's dead!"

And Lisa yelled.

Then there came a clumping, blundering noise from behind the hay barn and Miss Bell

felt something else that she had not felt for a long time – fear. She could not move.

Around the corner of the barn, skidding in short zig-zags and fierce little runs came Geoffrey. He blew at the ground. His head swung. He turned his red eyes on Miss Bell who at once forgot she was old and frail and gave a great spring behind the dairy door – and bolted it.

Geoffrey put his forehead very near the ground indeed and began slowly, slowly to swing his head, he began slowly, slowly to

scrape one of his front hooves backwards in a little trench. He gave a great bellow and prepared to charge.

Then quickly and quietly along the top of the wall from the direction of the hay barn came two black feet with two black ankles above them and The Kit above those. She skipped down out of sight into the hay field and pulled the gate wide open – with herself well behind it. Geoffrey stopped scraping his foot and stopped bellowing and slowly he lifted his head, blinked his crimson eyes and puffed a little down his nose. Then he sensibly trotted through.

The Kit bobbed up and shut the gate, was over it before Geoffrey could turn round, and found herself faced now with a wild and flying arms-aspread Miss Bell careering towards her like a huge, comforting pet goose. "Miss Bell," she said, "could you get Mother? She's halfway up the wall of the bull's hull and her macintosh and apron and scarf and that are all in the mire. She's clinging to the stones by her fingers and her toes are on the manger top and her eyes are all popping like a ferret. She can't speak for fright!

"I'm sorry," she said, "I just can't go back. I hate that mucky hull. I know I'm a sop and I don't suppose I'll ever get to London."

"And I dare say you won't," said Miss Bell, wrapping her up in her wings, "I dare say you won't. For I don't see how any of them can do without you."